Welcome to ALADDIN QUIX!

If you are looking for fast, fun-to-read stories with colorful characters, lots of kid-friendly humor, easy-to-follow action, entertaining story lines, and lively illustrations, then **ALADDIN QUIX** is for you!

But wait, there's more!

If you're also looking for stories with tables of contents; word lists; about-the-book questions; 64, 80, or 96 pages; short chapters; short paragraphs; and large fonts, then **ALADDIN QUIX** is *definitely* for you!

ALADDIN QUIX: The next step between ready to reads and longer, more challenging chapter books, for readers five to eight years old.

Read more ALADDIN QUIX books!

By Stephanie Calmenson

Our Principal Is a Frog!
Our Principal Is a Wolf!
Our Principal's in His Underwear!
Our Principal Breaks a Spell!

Royal Sweets
By Helen Perelman

Book 1: *A Royal Rescue*
Book 2: *Sugar Secrets*
Book 3: *Stolen Jewels*

A Miss Mallard Mystery
By Robert Quackenbush

Dig to Disaster
Texas Trail to Calamity
Express Train to Trouble
Stairway to Doom
Bicycle to Treachery
Gondola to Danger
Surfboard to Peril
Taxi to Intrigue

Little Goddess Girls
By Joan Holub and Suzanne Williams

Book 1: *Athena & the Magic Land*
Book 2: *Persephone & the Giant Flowers*
Book 3: *Aphrodite & the Gold Apple*

Little
GODDESS
Girls

Artemis & the Awesome Animals

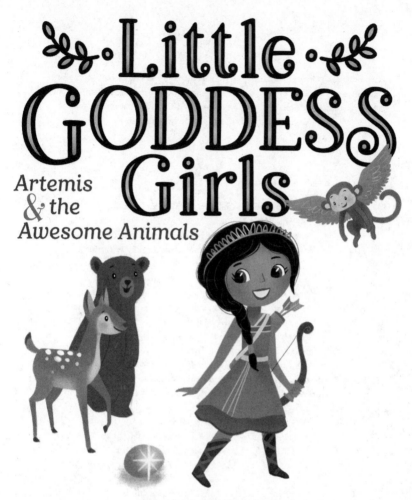

JOAN HOLUB &
SUZANNE WILLIAMS

ALADDIN QUIX

New York   London   Toronto   Sydney   New Delhi

ALADDIN QUIX
Simon & Schuster Children's Publishing Division
1230 Avenue of the Americas, New York, New York 10020
First Aladdin QUIX hardcover edition May 2020
Text copyright © 2020 by Joan Holub and Suzanne Williams
Illustrations copyright © 2020 by Yuyi Chen
Also available in an Aladdin QUIX paperback edition.
All rights reserved, including the right of reproduction in whole or in part in any form.
ALADDIN and the related marks and colophon are registered trademarks
of Simon & Schuster, Inc.
For information about special discounts for bulk purchases,
please contact Simon & Schuster Special Sales at 1-866-506-1949
or business@simonandschuster.com.
The Simon & Schuster Speakers Bureau can bring authors to your live event. For more
information or to book an event contact the Simon & Schuster Speakers Bureau
at 1-866-248-3049 or visit our website at www.simonspeakers.com.
Designed by Tiara Iandiorio
The illustrations for this book were rendered digitally.
The text of this book was set in Archer Medium.
Manufactured in the United States of America 0420 LAK
2 4 6 8 10 9 7 5 3 1
Library of Congress Control Number 2020932413
ISBN 978-1-5344-3115-7 (hc)
ISBN 978-1-5344-3114-0 (pbk)
ISBN 978-1-5344-3116-4 (eBook)

Cast of Characters

Artemis (AR•tih•miss):
A black-haired girl with a bow
and arrow

Athena (uh•THEE•nuh): A
brown-haired girl who travels to
magical Mount Olympus

Aphrodite (af•row•DYE•tee):
A golden-haired girl found in a
large seashell

Persephone (purr•SEFF•oh•nee):
A girl with flowers and leaves
growing in her hair and on her
dress

Oliver (AH•liv•er): Athena's white puppy

Zeus (ZOOSS): Most powerful of the Greek gods, who lives in Sparkle City and can grant wishes

Medusa (meh•DOO•suh): A mean mortal girl with snakes for hair, whose stare can zap mortals to stone

Gray Sisters (GRAY SISS•terz): Three talking chickens who know where to find Medusa

Hestia (HESS•tee•uh): A small, winged Greek goddess who helps Athena and her friends

Contents

1

Sparkly Tower

A huge magical peacock shook his blue tail feathers at **Artemis** and her three friends **Athena**, **Aphrodite**, and **Persephone**. **"Eek!"** Artemis squeaked in fear, dropping the silver arrow she held. She carried her bow and arrows everywhere.

"Don't be afraid," said the woman riding on the peacock's back. "He's a pet. He won't hurt you."

Athena's little white dog, **Oliver,**

barked as the woman and pea-cock walked away. ***"Woof! Woof!"***

Aphrodite smiled at him. "Too late to act brave now, Oliver."

"Yeah," said Persephone. "That peacock is gone."

"Or maybe when danger is past is the safest time to be brave," joked Artemis. She grabbed the arrow she had dropped and stuck it back in its **quiver**.

The other three girls giggled. They knew Artemis was scared of many things, including animals. She'd even been scared of Oliver at first!

Artemis had met the dog and her new friends here in the magical land of **Mount Olympus**. It was the tallest mountain in **Greece**. They had climbed it together, walking on the orange, blue, and pink Hello Brick Road. Now they stood in Sparkle City, at the very top of the mountain.

"I won't be a scaredy-cat for much longer, I hope," Artemis told her friends. "If **Zeus** gives me the gift of **courage**, I'll become brave!"

The girls had come here to Sparkle City to each ask Zeus for a special gift. He was the super-duper powerful king of the Greek **gods**. If anyone could grant their wishes, surely he could!

"Ooh! And I hope Zeus gives me the gift of good luck," said Persephone. "With good luck, I'll be able to help all plants grow strong."

Real leaves and flowers grew from Persephone's dress. And from her curly red hair, too. She loved plants, and they loved her. She did have **bad luck-itis**, though. For instance, some giant daisies had once tried to capture her to keep her as their friend forever!

Aphrodite flipped her long, golden hair. "Yeah! And if Zeus gives me the gift of **likability**, I won't be hard to like anymore."

Artemis already liked Aphrodite. She didn't mind that Aphrodite always said exactly what she thought. Still, Artemis knew that speaking without thinking first could cause trouble. Like when Aphrodite had once gotten herself trapped in a large shell in Wunderworld.

"I just hope Zeus will help me get back home," said Athena. Unlike the other girls, she didn't belong in this magic land. A strange storm had blown her to Mount Olympus from far away. Oliver had found her here, and they'd become pals. A pair of magical winged sandals that could really fly had found her too. Those wings fluttered now, lifting her a few inches off the ground before setting her back down.

Artemis looked up at the sky. "Let's walk faster, so we'll get to the tower before it's dark," she suggested. Being scared of the dark was another of her fears.

She and her friends punched their fists high. "Girl power. To the tower!" they shouted. The gleaming tower where Zeus lived stood at Sparkle City's center.

As the girls hurried toward it, they passed tidy little shops and houses. There were round ones, heart-shaped ones, and even some shaped like Xs. They were painted all the colors of the rainbow.

Happy people were everywhere. Some drove by on chariots pulled by unicorns or leopards. Children zoomed by on candy cane bikes. Some people rode upon the backs of dragons that puffed purple smoke!

Whoosh! Whizz!

Colorful fireworks crisscrossed the sky above the city. Oliver barked at them.

Aphrodite's blue eyes filled with delight. "I love how Sparkle City is so sparkly."

"Yeah! Even its flowers are," said Persephone. She waved to some sparkly pansies in a garden. They waved their petals back.

Soon the girls reached the tower. They looked up at it. Way, way up. It was very tall and shaped like a giant thunderbolt!

A nose appeared, poking out at them from the tower's front door. Two eyes and a mouth appeared too. The door had a face!

"Who goes there?" asked the face.

Athena clapped her hands. "How fun! Doors don't talk where I come from."

"That's strange!" said the door. Of course, many objects could speak in magical Mount Olympus.

"We are four friends, here to

see Zeus," Persephone explained quickly.

Artemis felt excited. They were so close to having their gift wishes granted!

"Yeah, so open up!" Aphrodite commanded.

The face frowned. "Nope. Zeus is too busy for you."

Oh no! thought Artemis.

As usual, Aphrodite had spoken without thinking. And she'd made the door mad.

Suddenly the wings on the heels of Athena's sandals fluttered again.

"**Wait!** Are those magic sandals?" the door asked her.

Athena nodded. "Yes."

"Hmm. Zeus will want to know about this. Come in!" said the door.

It swung itself open, and the girls marched inside with Oliver trotting behind them.

2

Zeus

"**Wow!**" said Aphrodite, looking around inside Zeus's thunderbolt tower. "It's so fancy!"

The zigzag tower walls were covered with swirls of glitter, and the floor was painted gold. Stairs went up all the way to its top. There were doors and windows here and there too.

Suddenly a big bunny with white fur appeared on the stairs. It hopped right up to the girls.

Artemis hopped backward to get away. "W-w-what do you want?" she asked it.

The bunny wiggled its fuzzy ears and pointed its paw at a door. "You can sleep in there. In the morning, you'll visit Zeus," it told them.

The girls' bedroom had bunk beds stacked four high. Each bed had a soft blanket and a heart-shaped pillow. A tall ladder leaned against the beds.

"Oliver can't climb. He and I better sleep on the bottom bunk," said Athena.

Artemis dashed up the ladder to claim the second bunk. Sleeping on the higher ones would be too scary for her.

Aphrodite and Persephone took the two top bunks. The girls fell asleep right away.

The next morning a yummy breakfast magically appeared in their room: thunderbolt-shaped pancakes! After they ate, the bunny took them to the **throne** room.

A jeweled throne sat at the room's center. And there was . . . a giant blue head floating around the room!

"Is that a balloon?" Persephone asked. It had black eyes and eyebrows, a nose, and a frowny mouth.

Artemis gulped. Balloons were one more thing she found scary. Because balloons could pop. This one was twice as big as she was tall. Its pop would be very loud!

Oliver growled at the balloon. ***"Grrr!"***

"Shhh," Athena told her dog. She picked him up and set him inside the book bag she carried. Oliver peeked out of its top flap to growl at the balloon some more.

Boing! Boing! The balloon bounced over to sit on the throne. "Behold! I am the super-duper powerful Zeus," the balloon boomed in a loud voice. "I'm king of the gods. Ruler of Mount Olympus!"

"Zeus is a *balloon*?" Aphrodite

said to her friends in surprise.

"Weird!" said Persephone.

Artemis hid behind her friends, hoping Zeus wouldn't notice her. No such luck.

"You. In the back. Scaredy-girl. Show yourself!" commanded Zeus. He sounded grumpy.

Oh no! This was bad luck. Had she caught Persephone's bad luck-itis? wondered Artemis. She didn't move. She couldn't. Because she was frozen. Zeus was *that* scary!

The other girls stepped to the

side a little, so Zeus could see her.

"Go on. Tell him what we want," Athena whispered.

The girls sent Artemis kind smiles to **encourage** her. Thinking of the word "encourage" reminded her of what she was here to get. And that was *courage*.

"Um . . . we want gifts," she told the balloon in a tiny voice.

"GIFTS?" Zeus boomed.

Artemis's knees shook as she nodded. "Mm-hmm. As in, help."

"Right. I need your help to get

back home," Athena explained to Zeus. "I don't belong in Mount Olympus. A storm brought me here by mistake."

"I seek the gift of likability," Aphrodite told him.

"I came to get a cure for my bad luck-itis," said Persephone.

The three girls looked at Artemis, waiting for her to speak up. Their encouraging smiles caused a strange, happy feeling to come over her. Almost a brave feeling.

Then Zeus eyed Artemis again.

"And you? What do you want?" he boomed.

Her brave feeling melted away. "Nothing," she squeaked. Oh no! She'd missed her chance!

The balloon bounced off the throne and around the room. *Boing! Boing!* Then it stopped right in front of the girls, frowning.

"NO GIFTS!" Zeus yelled. "I'm too busy to help you. Some **goddesses** and gods called Titans are trying to take over Mount Olympus. And—"

Just then, Zeus noticed Athena's sandals. His eyes got wide. "Okay, I'll give you the gifts you want," he said.

Artemis blinked, surprised. "You will?"

"Yes," said Zeus. "But first you must do something for me."

"Sure!" said Persephone.

"Anything!" said Aphrodite.

"No problem," said Athena.

Artemis nodded. "What is it?"

The Zeus balloon grinned. "You must stop **Medusa** from making trouble. Forever."

All four girls stared at him in shock. Everyone knew about Medusa. Green snakes grew on her head instead of hair. And Artemis was *super afraid* of snakes. Plus Medusa could turn you to stone with a zap from her eyes.

"W-what? How are we supposed to do that?" Artemis dared to ask Zeus.

His smile turned upside down. "That's your problem. Now shoo! And don't come back until you have proof that Medusa won't cause any more trouble!"

"But—" Artemis tried to say.

"Go! Now! OR ELSE!" yelled Zeus.

The four friends turned and ran out of the tower.

3

Stopping Medusa

The girls kept running until they reached a tall glass wall dotted with jewels. This wall surrounded Sparkle City. There was only one way to get through it. Luckily, the girls had discovered the secret.

Aphrodite took a walnut-size gold apple from her pocket. She'd found it on their last trip to this city. She pulled up on the apple's stem. *Click!* The apple hummed a tune.

Artemis and Persephone both grabbed on to one of Aphrodite's arms. With Oliver safe in her book bag, Athena held on to Aphrodite's other arm. Then Aphrodite pressed the gold apple against the glass wall. They all held their breath and stepped forward. The glass began to ripple around them.

They magically passed through the wall! Now they were outside Sparkle City again, standing on the Hello Brick Road.

Artemis's shoulders slumped. "There's no way we can stop Medusa. So I guess I'll have to keep on being a scaredy-girl."

"And I'll never become likable," said Aphrodite.

"I'll always have bad luck-itis," said Persephone.

"And I'll never get back home," said Athena. She looked

like she was about to cry.

Artemis felt most sorry for her. It wasn't fair that Athena was stuck in this magic land where she didn't belong. She should get her wish, to return home!

"Wait! Let's not give up yet," Artemis said. "Does anyone know where Medusa lives?"

Aphrodite shrugged. "In a castle on Mount Olympus." But none of them knew exactly where her castle was.

"Go ask the **Gray Sisters**.

They'll know," suggested a voice. It was coming from a tall Hello Brick Road signpost!

The girls turned to look at the talking sign. "Where can we find these Gray Sisters?" Athena asked eagerly.

"Just walk along the Hello Brick Road, making chicken noises," said the signpost. "And they'll find *you*."

"Chicken noises?" Persephone repeated in surprise.

"You know, clucking and stuff," said the sign.

"It's worth a try," said Athena.

The four girls thanked the sign and headed down the road. As they walked, they flapped their arms like chicken wings. *"Cluck! Cluck!"* they called out. It felt silly, but it was also kind of fun!

Minutes later three real chickens flew to sit atop a fence along the road. Their feathers were gray.

"Are you the Gray Sisters?" Artemis asked them.

The first chicken flapped its wings. *"Cluck! Cluckity-cluck-cluck!"* The other two stayed silent. Likely because the first chicken was the only one that had a beak!

"Sorry. We don't understand chicken talk," said Athena.

But Artemis had understood. "They said yes, they are the Gray Sisters," she told her friends. "They can only speak one at a time because they have to share their beak."

The other three girls looked at her strangely.

"You understand chicken talk?" asked Aphrodite.

Artemis nodded. "Sure, I can understand lots of animals."

"Wow," said Persephone. "Just . . . wow."

"Can you ask them where Medusa is?" Athena asked Artemis. "And how we could stop her from making trouble?"

"Umm," said Artemis. Those chickens' sharp claws had her feeling a bit chicken about asking.

The chickens had been listening, though. The second one took the beak and put it on its face. "*Cluck! Squawk! Squawkity-cluck!*" it said.

Artemis pointed at a field beyond the fence. "She said if we walk across that field, we'll come to a forest," she explained. "That's where Medusa's castle is."

"But we'll be in danger if we leave the Hello Brick Road," Athena said to Artemis. "A tiny flying goddess we met named **Hestia** said so."

"Yeah, the road is safe. Once we step off it, Medusa could trick us," added Persephone.

The second chicken passed the beak to the third chicken. *"Bawk! Squawk!"* said chicken number three. Then it laid a silver egg atop the fence.

"It said that the egg it laid is named Perseus. It's for us," Artemis explained to her friends. "It's supposed to help us stop Medusa like Zeus asked."

The girls all looked toward the field. They saw a green glow.

"Think that glow could be coming from Medusa's castle?" asked Aphrodite.

"Let's go find out," said

Athena. "Leaving this road is dangerous. But it's our only hope of getting Zeus to help us." She climbed over the fence and toward the field.

Persephone and Aphrodite followed her.

Artemis turned back to the chickens. They had flown away! Only the egg remained. She put it in her pocket and climbed the fence too.

"Wait up!" she called.

The girls stuck close together as they walked through the field toward the green glow. They hadn't gone far when they heard a flapping sound overhead.

Persephone pointed up at the sky. "Hey, look at those weird hairy birds!"

"Those aren't birds!" yelled Aphrodite. "They're flying monkeys!"

The winged monkeys swooped down. Before the girls could race back to safety on the road, the monkeys carried them away, leaving Oliver behind.

4

Captured!

Soon they came to a glowing, green castle deep in the forest. The monkeys set the girls down on the front steps. And there stood Medusa.

"You sent those monkeys to bring us here, didn't you?"

Aphrodite asked the snaky-haired girl.

"Yep! *Eee-heh-heh!* Gotcha now! Once you stepped off the Hello Brick Road, it was easy." Medusa did a little happy dance.

When she stopped, she fixed her eyes on the winged monkeys. **Zap!** Her gaze turned them to stone! Next she turned her stone-gaze on Athena, Aphrodite, Persephone, and Artemis.

Oh no! The girls did a group hug and hoped for the best.

Zap!

Nothing happened. "We didn't turn to stone!" said Persephone.

Looking surprised and mad about this, Medusa pointed at Athena. "Give me those sandals!" Her snakes flicked their red, forked tongues at the girls.

"**No!**" said Athena. "You'll use them to make trouble."

Medusa smiled a sneaky smile. "Okay, no problem. Come into my castle, and we'll chat."

The stone monkeys herded the

girls toward the castle door. When the girls came close, Medusa stuck out her foot. She tripped Athena!

As Athena fell backward, one of her magic sandals came untied. It fell off her foot. Medusa tried to grab the loose sandal, but it escaped!

Medusa chased after it. "Come back here, you silly sandal! Your magic powers should belong to me! They'll make me as powerful as any goddess."

Athena jumped to her feet. "Stop her!" she called to Artemis, Persephone, and Aphrodite.

"Army, rise up!" Medusa shouted. At once, large animal-shaped stones popped up from the ground to join the stone monkeys. There were life-size deer, wolves, bears, giraffes, hippos, and more. *Stomp! Stomp!* Medusa's army marched in a circle around the girls, chanting.

"Once we were animals. Now we are stone.

"Changed by Medusa who rules from her throne.

"All of her orders we must obey.

"We do what she tells us to, day after day."

Artemis and her friends were trapped. **"Let us go, or else!"** she warned.

Medusa just laughed and kept chasing the sandal. "Or else what? You don't scare me or my army."

Artemis remembered the Perseus

egg. The third gray chicken had said it would stop Medusa.

Though she didn't see how it could do that, she reached into her pocket. Her fingers curled around the silver egg. But as she pulled it out, her elbow bumped the wing of a stone monkey behind her.

"Ow!" She dropped the egg, and it rolled away.

It came to a stop at Medusa's feet. "Hey, what's this?" Medusa picked up the egg. She lifted it close to study it.

Zap!

Suddenly Medusa's face went stiff. So did her snaky hair. And all the rest of her too. Holding the egg up to her face, she now stood as still as a statue. Because she had turned into one!

Artemis, her friends, and the whole army gazed in shock at the stone Medusa statue.

"That egg was so shiny that Medusa saw herself in it," said Aphrodite.

"Like in a mirror," said Athena.

"Her stone-gaze bounced off it," said Persephone.

"And she zapped herself into a statue!" said Artemis.

Just then, Athena's missing sandal flew back to her. She lifted her bare foot. The sandal slipped onto it and laced itself up to her knee again.

Stomp! Stomp!

Medusa's army was again heading straight for the girls.

Even though she was scared, Artemis stood up to them. "Oh, no you don't! You're not going to hurt my friends!" She pulled a silver arrow from her quiver and strung it in her bow. "Halt, or I'll shoot!"

"Wait!" a hippo called out. "We only want to thank you. You have freed us from Medusa's spell!"

Then Artemis saw that the animals weren't stone anymore. When Medusa changed to stone, they had changed back into normal animals with fur, feathers, or scales.

The four girls looked at one another and smiled. They'd done it! They'd stopped Medusa!

"Can you help us?" Athena asked the animals. "We need proof that Medusa won't cause trouble anymore."

"To show Zeus in Sparkle City," Persephone explained.

The animals nodded. "We'll carry the statue there for you to show him."

"Thanks," said Artemis. Now that they weren't under Medusa's power, these animals were pretty **awesome**!

Some of them tried to pick up the statue. They grunted and groaned.

"It's too heavy to carry to Sparkle City," the bears decided.

"Too heavy to fly it there either," said the winged monkeys.

Giving up, they set the statue

back down. It fell over. **Crack!**
One of her hair snakes broke off!

Athena picked up the broken snake. "Look, the tip of its tongue is shaped like an M, for Medusa."

"Perfect!" said Artemis. "That shows that it's no ordinary snake. It could only be Medusa's. It's proof we turned her to stone."

"Hooray! Let's go show Zeus," said Persephone.

The girls told the animals goodbye, then

crossed the field to get back to the Hello Brick Road. Partway there, Oliver met them. He jumped around, happy to see them again.

Meanwhile, Artemis looked over her shoulder, back toward Medusa's statue. Her eyes went wide.

Seeing her look of surprise, Aphrodite asked, "What is it?"

"Oh, nothing. I thought I saw one of Medusa's snakes move," said Artemis. "But I'm sure I was just imagining it. Let's go."

5

Thunderbolt Tower

The girls climbed to the top of Mount Olympus again. Using Aphrodite's small gold apple, they passed through the glass wall and into Sparkle City. They went right to Zeus's tower. Soon they were standing in his throne room.

"We turned Medusa to stone," Athena told the Zeus balloon.

"Where is your proof?" Zeus boomed, bouncing around. Oliver growled at the balloon's string like he'd done before.

And also like before, Zeus's loud voice scared Artemis. It must have scared Athena too, because she dropped the stone snake. Luckily, Artemis caught it before it hit the floor and broke even more. *Eww!* She didn't like snakes, not even stone ones. Shaking with fright, she tossed the stone snake onto the seat of Zeus's throne. "H-h-here."

Zeus bounced over to look at it. "That's your proof? A long, skinny rock?" he asked. He did a flip, then spun around.

"It's one of Medusa's hair snakes," said Persephone.

"We turned her into a statue," said Aphrodite.

"Hmph! That could be any old snake that Medusa herself

changed to stone," said Zeus.

"No . . ." Athena tried to explain about the special M-shaped tongue. But Zeus wouldn't listen.

"Grrr." Suddenly Oliver leaped at the balloon's string. He grabbed it in his teeth. Then he ran around the room, pulling the balloon behind him.

"Let go!" the Zeus balloon yelled. As he was dragged

through the air, Zeus huffed and puffed. His balloon head grew bigger. And bigger. Soon it would fill the room!

"If we don't get out of here, that balloon is going to squish us all!" Aphrodite shouted to the others.

She was right, thought Artemis. But they couldn't leave Oliver behind to get squished! Quickly she pulled a silver arrow from her quiver. She set it in her bow. **Ready. Aim. Fire!** *POP!* Her arrow burst the balloon. As air rushed out of it, a boy tumbled out too!

"Ow!" the boy said as he landed on the floor.

The girls all stared at him. He looked about eight years old, the same age as them. He had black hair and wore a tunic. There was a thunderbolt on his belt.

"Who are you?" Artemis asked.

"Nobody," the boy mumbled.

The girls went closer.

"You're Zeus, aren't you?" guessed Athena.

The boy's face turned red. "Okay, yeah. The super-duper powerful king of the gods. That's me."

"But a kid can't rule Mount Olympus," said Persephone.

"A *godboy* can," Zeus said proudly. "And I *am* a godboy. With magic powers. I don't know how to use all of them yet. But I'm learning." He lowered his voice. "Please don't tell anybody, though. Troublemakers might attack Sparkle City if they think I'm weak."

Artemis gulped. Titans sounded *very* scary.

"Medusa really is a statue now. So, please, can we have our gifts?" Athena reminded him.

Zeus sighed. "I'll try. Tell me what you want again?"

"I want the gift of likability," Aphrodite said quickly. "I will always say what I truly believe. I just don't want to cause hurt feelings or big trouble when I don't mean to."

Zeus thought for a minute. Then he went to the closet in the corner of the room. He got out a bag. From it, he pulled a small, gleaming crown. He placed the crown on Aphrodite's head. A pink, shell-shaped jewel on its front twinkled.

"From now on, this thinking crown will remind you to think before you speak," he said to her.

Aphrodite smiled. "I can hardly wait to see if it works!"

Zeus turned to Persephone. "How about you?"

"I have bad luck-itis," Persephone said. "Do you have a cure for me?"

Zeus thought for another minute. Then he dug in his bag and pulled out seven small seeds. He tossed them into her daisy-filled hair. Instantly they sprouted into four-leaf clovers.

"There. That should help. Clovers with four or more leaves are lucky. And seven is a very lucky number too," he told her.

Persephone jumped up and down, clapping. "I'm going to use my new good luck to help plants grow." She touched a drooping daisy in her hair. It sprang up straight. And twice the normal size!

"Oops! I think I made it a bit *too* big," said Persephone.

Aphrodite opened her mouth to speak. Then she cocked her head, thinking first. "Don't worry. You'll get better at growing things, I'm sure." Her eyes got round. "Wow, that was a nice thing I just said. This crown must be working!"

Now Zeus turned to Artemis. "And you? What gift do you seek?"

For a minute Artemis froze in

fear. But then she looked at her friends and saw their smiles. Their *encouraging* smiles. Suddenly words rushed out of her. "I don't want to be a scaredy-girl anymore."

Zeus looked surprised. "What are you afraid of?"

"Um, everything?" Artemis told him. "I need some courage."

"But you already stood up to Medusa's army, remember?" Athena said. "That was very brave."

"I didn't *feel* brave, though. Not in my heart," said Artemis.

"Aha! That gives me an idea." Zeus dug in his bag and pulled out a necklace with a heart-shaped ruby. "Wear this. Touch the ruby if you ever feel scared. It will remind you that you *do* have a brave heart."

"Oh, thank you!" Artemis put

on the necklace. Already feeling braver, she bravely asked Zeus, "What about Athena's gift?"

They all turned to look at Athena.

Gifts

"It would truly be a gift if you could send me back home. I don't belong here in this magic land," Athena told Zeus.

Zeus sighed. "I know. I caused the storm that brought you here by mistake. When I saw you wore the magic sandals, I knew you could help us fight Medusa. Those sandals would only let someone very special wear them. I'm not sure how to send you back home, though."

"Oh," Athena said sadly.

No fair! thought Artemis. "Isn't there anything in your bag that could take her back? Maybe you could magic up another wind?" she asked Zeus.

"Hmm. Magic? Wind? That's it!" Zeus pulled another balloon

from his bag. Then he led the girls upstairs and out onto the tower roof. There, he held the open end of the balloon up to catch a passing magic wind.

Once the balloon had puffed up to be huge, Zeus held it out to Athena. "This should fly you home."

"Oh, thank you!" said Athena. Quickly she hugged her friends goodbye. "I'll miss you guys so, so much." They hugged her back.

Then Athena picked up Oliver and gave him a big hug too. "I'll miss you, too," she told him. "But you belong here on Mount Olympus."

She handed him to Artemis, trying hard not to cry. "Take care of him for me?"

"I will," Artemis promised. Her fingers touched the ruby heart. Yesterday she would have been too scared to be in charge of a pet. But not anymore.

Athena turned back to Zeus. But before she could grab the balloon's string, a big gust of wind came by. **Whoosh!** The balloon was pulled high into the air, and Zeus with it!

"Sorry," he called. "Don't know how to come back. I'm still learning to control my powers!" The girls could only watch as he and the balloon blew away and out of sight.

"Now I'll never get home," Athena wailed.

Like a ray of hope, a light suddenly began to blink in the air above them. A tiny, glowing fairylike goddess appeared to them.

"Hestia!" Persephone, Aphrodite, and Athena exclaimed.

So that's who this was, thought Artemis. She'd never met the goddess before now.

"I can help you," Hestia said

to Athena. "I'm the goddess of the home, after all."

"You are? I didn't know that," Athena said in wonder.

Hestia nodded. "I have even bigger news. **You are all goddess girls!**"

"Huh?" The girls looked at each other in surprise.

"But we don't have magic powers," said Artemis.

Hestia zipped back and forth in the air. "Yes, you do. But, like Zeus, you'll need to learn what they are and how to use them. This will take time. Practice well. Mount Olympus will need your help again. Medusa isn't the only troublemaker around here."

Just then, Hestia's light started blinking again. Speaking fast, she told Athena, "I don't know every-thing your magic sandals can do. But I know they can take you home. And bring you back here. Now, click your heels together three times and say this:

"'*Although sometimes friends*

must part, they're never far away. Home and friends live in your heart. You'll meet again one day!'

"To return to Mount Olympus in the future, click your heels and say:

"*'Magic sandals, whisk me high. To Mount Olympus, I will fly.'*"

With that, Hestia blinked away.

"We're goddesses!" Aphrodite exclaimed.

"Yippee!" They all jumped up and down with excitement.

Learning about our magic

powers and how to use them will be super fun. No matter how long it takes! thought Artemis.

But now it was time for Athena to go. She looked happy to be going home, but sad to leave them. **"We'll miss you!"** said Persephone.

"Yes, so much," added Aphrodite.

"Come back soon!" said Artemis.

"Woof!" barked Oliver. He lifted his paw to say goodbye.

"Bye! I'll miss you all too," Athena called to them.

Quickly she clicked her winged heels together three times. Then she repeated the words Hestia had given her.

Whoosh! Suddenly a strong, sparkly wind whipped up. A new storm lifted Athena off her feet. It blew her high in the sky.

Like magic, she was whisked away from Mount Olympus!

Minutes later the storm ended.

Athena floated down to stand on the sidewalk in front of a small white house. The words had worked. She was home again!

Right then, her school bus drove by. So it must be afternoon. But what day was it? she wondered.

"*Woof! Woof!*"

Was that Oliver barking? No. It wasn't her real puppy. It was the dog she'd created for her Happy

Perky Pets game. She spotted the tablet she'd been playing the game on. She'd dropped it there before the first storm whisked her away.

Athena picked up the tablet. It was still turned on. She checked the date on the screen. It was still the same day she'd left! Only a few minutes had passed since she'd gone to Mount Olympus.

I guess home time must pass much slower than magic time, she realized.

She skipped up the sidewalk to

her front door. Her trip to Mount Olympus had been amazing. She'd found out she was a goddess girl! She had made three new best friends. And gotten a pet, too!

Athena smiled down at her magic sandals. Someday soon they would carry her back to Mount Olympus. But for now she opened her front door.

"Mom!" she called out happily. **"I'm home!"**

Word List

awesome (AWE•sum): Great

bad luck-itis (BAD luck•I•tiss):
A made-up kind of bad luck that
spreads from person to person

courage (KER•idge): Bravery

encourage (in•KER•idge): Give help
or support

goddesses (GOD•ess•iz): Girls or
women with magic powers

gods (GODZ): Boys or men with
magic powers

Greece (GREES): A country on the continent of Europe

Greek mythology (GREEK mith•AH•luh•jee): Stories people in **Greece** made up long ago to explain things they didn't understand about their world

likability (like•uh•BILL•ih•tee): The state of being easy to like

Mount Olympus (MOWNT oh•LIHM•pus): Tallest mountain in Greece

quiver (KWI•ver): A bag for arrows

throne (THROHN): A royal chair

Questions

1. What emojis would you use to represent Zeus, Artemis, Aphrodite, Athena, Persephone, and Hestia? Why?

2. Do you think Medusa will figure out how to un-stone herself someday? If so, how?

3. Hestia tells Athena, Persephone, Aphrodite, and Artemis that they all have magic powers that they will learn to use. What magic powers have already been hinted at?

Authors' Note

Some of the ideas in the Little Goddess Girls books come from **Greek mythology**. Artemis was the goddess of animals and the moon, and was very good at archery. Her special animals were dogs and deer! We also borrowed a few ideas from *The Wonderful Wizard of Oz* by L. Frank Baum. While there are some similarities, we've added a lot of action and our own ideas. We hope you enjoy reading the Little Goddess Girls books!

—*Joan Holub and Suzanne Williams*